ZAK ZOO

and the
HECTIC HOUSE

Reading Consultant: Prue Goodwin, Lecturer in literacy and children's books

ORCHARD BOOKS
338 Euston Road, London NW1 3BH
Orchard Books Australia
Level 17/207 Kent Street, Sydney, NSW 2000

First published in 2012
First paperback publication in 2013

ISBN 978 1 40831 333 6 (hardback)
ISBN 978 1 40831 341 1 (paperback)

A CIP catalogue record for this book is available from the British Library.

1 3 5 7 9 10 8 6 4 2 (hardback)
1 3 5 7 9 10 8 6 4 2 (paperback)

Printed in China

Orchard Books is a division of Hachette Children's Books,
an Hachette UK company.
www.hachette.co.uk

and the
HECTIC HOUSE

Justine Smith • Clare Elsom

ORCHARD

Zak Zoo lives at Number One, Africa Avenue.
His mum and dad are away on
safari, so his animal family is looking
after him. Sometimes things get a little . . .

. . . WILD!

Pam

Emily

Dad

Mum

Zak

Nanny
Hilda

The Nesbits

Bob

Tom

Mia (Zak's best friend)

Grace

Cressida

One Wednesday night, Zak Zoo
was pushed out of his bed by lots
of sleeping animals!

Zak got up and went downstairs, stepping over more snoring creatures as he went. He loved living with his animal family, but the house was getting very busy.

Everyone had to take turns to eat breakfast, because there wasn't room at the table for them all.

Zak's mum and dad liked to send him presents. They liked to send him new members for his animal family, even though the house was full.

Muddy Base Camp,
River Bank Rise,
Africa

Dear Zak,

Here is a rare spectacled frog.

He is very shy. He likes the damp.

Love, Mum and Dad.

Zak took the frog to the
bathroom. It was getting very
crowded in there.

"We need a bigger house,"
said Zak.

That night, the sock drawer was too crowded for Pam. She decided to go next door to the house where Mr and Mrs Nesbit lived. She hoped the Nesbits had a big bed, with plenty of room in it for a friendly python.

The Nesbits' bed looked very

comfortable. Pam slithered onto

it and went to sleep.

In the middle of the night,

Mr Nesbit felt a tickle on his toes.

He switched on the lamp, and let
out a scream.

"Ssss," said Pam politely, but
Mr Nesbit got a terrible fright.

Mr Nesbit called Zak and asked

him to pick up his python.

"I am so sorry," said Zak.

"We need a bigger house."

The problem was getting urgent.

That night, it was Grace who fell
out of the crowded bed. Ouch!

Grace decided that she would
go next door, too. Pam had told
her about the big bed, which
had plenty of room in it for
a gorgeous gorilla.

Grace climbed into the Nesbits'
bed, stretched out, and fell asleep.
In the middle of the night,
Mr Nesbit felt a tickle on his nose.

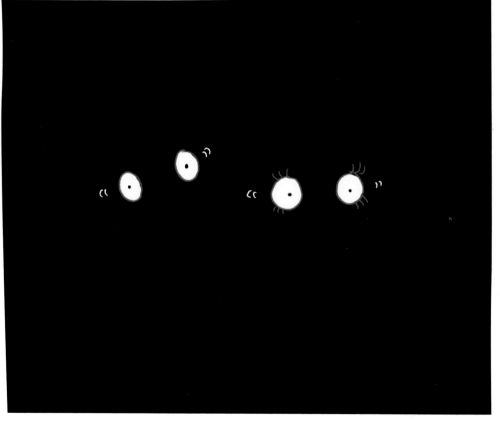

He switched on the lamp and got
another terrible fright.

Mr Nesbit grabbed the phone and called Zak.

"I am so sorry," Zak said. "I will come over right away."

After he had taken Grace home,

Zak rang his best friend, Mia.

"I need your help," he said.

"I need to find a bigger house."

"OK," said Mia. "But can it wait

until the morning? I'm sleeping!"

She went back to sleep.

The next day, Zak and Mia went to see the estate agent.

"How many bedrooms do you need?" the estate agent asked.

"About thirty," said Zak.

"What?" said the estate agent.

"How big is your family?"

"Quite big," said Zak. "There's one python, one iguana, one elephant, one . . ."

"We sell houses," said the estate
agent, "not zoos."
So Zak had to go back to his
old house.

That night, Cressida decided to explore next door as well.

Half an hour later, Mr Nesbit felt something move in his bath.

The shock of finding a crocodile in his bath was too much for Mr Nesbit. He fainted! His wife called the ambulance.

When Mr Nesbit was back from hospital, Zak went next door to see him. Cressida came too. "How are you feeling, Mr Nesbit?" called Zak. But nobody replied.

"Please let us in," said Zak.

"Cressida would like to say sorry."

But the Nesbits just passed a note

under the door.

Dear Zak,

We are going on a very long
holiday to a desert island.
It's the doctor's orders.
Goodbye for ever!

Best wishes,

Mr and Mrs Nesbit

The Nesbits' house stayed empty
for months. Nobody wanted to live
next to a family of wild animals.
Then Mia had a brilliant idea.
She wrote to ask the Nesbits if Zak's
family could stay in their house.
They wrote back, saying "Yes"!

Zak made some changes to the Nesbits' house, and his animal family moved in.

Zak wrote to the Nesbits every month:

Dear Mr and Mrs Nesbit,

We are still looking after your house.
We had to cut a hole in the roof for the giraffe.
But don't worry. The rain doesn't come in.

Best wishes,
Zak Zoo

But the Nesbits never wrote back.

Written by Justine Smith • Illustrated by Clare Elsom

Zak Zoo and the School Hullabaloo	978 1 40831 337 4
Zak Zoo and the Peculiar Parcel	978 1 40831 338 1
Zak Zoo and the Seaside SOS	978 1 40831 339 8
Zak Zoo and the Unusual Yak	978 1 40831 340 4
Zak Zoo and the Hectic House	978 1 40831 341 1
Zak Zoo and the Baffled Burglar	978 1 40831 342 8
Zak Zoo and the TV Crew	978 1 40831 343 5
Zak Zoo and the Birthday Bang	978 1 40831 344 2

All priced at £4.99

Orchard Books are available from all good bookshops,
or can be ordered from our website: www.orchardbooks.co.uk,
or telephone 01235 827702, or fax 01235 827703.

Prices and availability are subject to change.